Alaska

Evening Pearls

Shadowman

The Wolf

Erotic

Short

Stories

©by Silkfairy, ErotiCastle 2016

Erotic Short Stories

© by Silkfairy, ErotiCastle, 2016, first edition printed in Feb. 2016 , published by BOD, Book on Demand, stories originally written in 2000 by Silkfairy.

***

ISBN 978-3-7392-3630-8

Table of Contents

Alaska

He stood there, eyes closed, deeply taking in the icy freshness of the damp mountain ridge that was ready to be taken like the cleavage of a woman, calling, a snowy path winding upwards like her long legs clinging to the massive intensity of the dark Alaskan sky, hanging deeply over her body, in intense, powerful movements, pushing, snowdunes shifting, giving her a different appearance now, her wide breasts almost pressed down, adapting to the rhythm of that snowstorm that was moulding her, towering over her, taking her, penetrating her till the moment of bizarre surprise, then she would let go, the winding path disappearing, overshadowed by desire and rapture, yielding, until the skies fell down on her, melting into her, letting her mountain explode into it, till his spirit cried out, pressing his loins deep down into the fantastic formation of hills and valleys, ever changing, and yet so eternal.

The man stopped, looked up, and smiled to himself, laughing out loud to the daydream that had brushed his clear thoughts, that used to function, to focus, and were trained to survive in the whites of the virginal polar desert, where no such dreams were allowed in the view of the next storm that was announcing itself by that brittleness of glassy air, biting his face and making his tense body shiver. Why did he set out for this adventure, what was he to encounter, wasn't it too much to take, so far away from home. He stretched out his arms, opened his mouth and let out a resolute yell that resulted from that ultimate human urge to make that woman his own, taking her away from that panting snowstorm that whipped over her body in raging clouds now, the white of her rounded breasts now glistening with the spume of a heavenly rampant whim to defeat her in gushes of icy cascades, filling every opening of her outstretched body, her silhouette now hardly visible but like a flaming blurred shadow against the falling red and golden sun. He could feel the stifling cold breath of the other while he hurried to get closer to that singing voice he could make out from under the constant pumping of the towering snowmasses, now ready to ejaculate their seed into the huge crater that to him seemed like the open vagina of a woman, helpless, yet at the same time praying in readiness for that wild male possessive urge that would make her forever his.

My God, he murmured, while he laboured upwards, hardly seeing the winding path that lead to shelter, right there where the darker patch of snow masses of the woman's sleek body covered a silent valley, weakly illuminated by some tiny lights that from afar looked like flickering fireflies, testimony of the sparks of orgasm, after which the storm would have subsided, to give way to relief, and a relaxed rest, where he would then be able to bury his hot face into that dark velvet orchid, one last kiss before he would drift to sleep, by the warm lights of shelter that his comrades had kindled to prepare a wintry night at the station. His ears were filled by the emptiness after the imaginary orchestral orgasm that had subsided into those contracting waves that nearly sucked him in, so that he had to push all his weight against those spiral movements to hold, move on, further into the direction of where the lights were dancing and flickering. Panting against the storm, he was crouching for a moment, then getting up his feet again to continue. One last vision of the sun, and the outline of her body seemed to shine as if she had just received that inner glee brought forth by the golden rain spurting out into her softness. Her hair seemed like orange flames seaming the horizon, and green diluted eyes seemed to touch him while he was watching and caressing her long sensuous neck with his fingertips from where he was standing.

With a smile on his lips, he reached the camp, then an unbelievable glance, a groan, while he touched his pulsating erection, so hard, that it almost hurt. "Danae! I am coming".

<u>**E**vening Pearls</u>

She stood in front of the large brass mirror looking closely at her reflection that was slightly blurred due to the flickering flames of the open fireplace behind her shapely figure which were being reflected in the mirror, too. She was ransacking her mind for new inspiration to bring forth something to put on canvas, something to be worth painting, something which would involve all her senses. She only could paint naked, , and only when there was enough of that strange energy inside so that she had to grab her brush that very moment to catch something of that prescious streams of mind jewels that were about to materialize and let her emerge in the holy process of creation. Her nudity always added to that urge and desire, and usually, she would paint a fantasy of her erotic dreams arising of which she knew that her brush was the only tool to give them the shape of her innermost longing. The flickering fire warmed her smooth skin, and the golden sparks were dancing in the mirror to make her image look like the swaying ocean waves, when the evening sunrays were mingling with the spray and spume of the tide rolling in towards the shoreline with both, tenderness and intensity.

She halfway closed her eyes, taking the end of the paintbrush between her teeth as if she wanted to smoke a cigar, chewing at it, turning it round, then gently feeling the hard hairs of the brush against her chest. She needed to feel, and imagine. The fire and evening sun constantly changed her body silhouette into little dancing flames nourished by the pressing touch of the brush against her soft flesh. She was thinking too hard, she noticed, she was still so controlled, no way to make the spirits touch her tonight and endow her with their gifts. She opened her eyes and her glance met that beautiful red rose that was about to fully open so that the velvet petals looked like a woman's secret parts when she was ready for love. She opened the colours she would need this evening. The intense smell always made her feel dazed, even thrilled. It was like a sensual experience, that string of those prescious and rare pearls of inspiration, to be gently put around her neck by the hands of her lover.

She went over to the chest of drawers and opened it, holding a shimmering pearl necklace in her small hands. They felt cool against her hands and thighs that were still warm from standing in front of the brass mirror while the flames had tenderly touched her back and buttocks. She felt aroused, excited. Yes, it would work. She closed her eyes again, feeling the glowing pearls, rubbing them into her responding skin, then, slowly, she held the ends of the necklace between her fingers, walking back again to the brass mirror. She watched herself, and slowly opened her legs. She could feel the juice gathering inside her, and her body started to get tense, sending out its own rays right through her like electricity. Softly she guided the string of pearls between her legs, holding one end with her left hand, then turning her head slightly to watch her right hand hold the end of the necklace, with part of the string hidden in the cavities of her vagina that were now wet with excitement. Slowly, she moved the necklace between her spread legs, enjoying the touches of each individual pearl that was massaging her clitoris that already began to harden. She was silently moaning, her mouth half open with arousal, her nipples erect and wanting. She stood there, trancelike, until she could feel the pearls as hard as if they were one with her clitoris, as if that sensual part of her was one of those secret pearls, hidden in a beautiful shell. She stopped rubbing, pressing one pearl against her clitoris instead. She sighed with pleasure when she could feel her desire rise even more. Soon, that very moment would be reached when she would stop pressing the pearl but gently touch that tip of her clitoris with her own finger. She put aside the necklace, and lay down on the hard wooden floorboards. Her legs slightly apart, she felt herself to be moist, ready for relief. With slow, rotating movements, she started to masturbate. If someone was observing her through the window of her loft, he would see directly onto her fingers rubbing her clitoris. She opened her legs widely, and now her vagina looked like that velvet rose that was fully open, drinking the sunrays, with single drops of dew dripping slowly along the petals. She had a vision of a man standing over her for a short while, but she could not stop rubbing herself now. Then she was aware that there really was someone in her room, intensely observing her, with dark desire in his amber eyes. She suddenly felt the paintbrush against her thighs, then between her legs. She gasped with lust, when the heavy body of the man pressed itself against hers, to make her feel his erection against her belly first, and then, against her vagina. His warm large hands clung to her buttocks, then caressed and squeezed her hips and bum. His right hand slowly moved one of her thighs. With a jerk, he entered the soft flesh until his hard penis filled all of her. With rhythmical movements, his pelvis was pressing her to the ground even harder, until she shrieked with pleasure. She slightly lifted her knees but his body weight pressed her down again. He was close to his own orgasm, when he could feel her come in short spasms, her juice inviting him to give himself relief. He groaned, when his seed spurted into her, mingling with her wetness. They held each other firmly for a long moment.

She looked up, smiling, pulling his head and face down against her breasts, feeling his thick hair, touching his closed eyelids.

Yes, she knew what she would paint tonight...

Shadowman

One day, she felt something had to change... She was full of the wildest fantasies, and yet there was no suitable man to fulfill her innermost needs. At nights, she lay away, being full of unrest, of craving, and of anticipation. The shadows in her bedroom were dancing and teasing her, tempting her, adding to her desire to feel in flesh, what her mind imagined. Yes, her flesh felt like hot fire, there was a burning longing in her heart, and between her legs, and when she ran her soft fingers along her smooth thighs, she sighed, feeling the urge to be united with her lover. He was there, outside, somewhere, teasing her by his absence, still hiding, knowing that there would be the right time, to meet her, smile at her, and do those things with her she so deeply desired...

One night, she felt that need in her rising again, yet something was different. She did not imagine her secret lover's touch, she could feel his hands on her sleek body, caressing her, gently stroking, groping her small breasts, twisting her nipples, until they were erect, and ready to make love with that man, she could not see but smell, and hear, and taste, and feel. Yes, finally, he was there, he had known it was time to come, yet he was also naughty, he had come to take her in her sleep, gently first, teasing like those shadows that were there, all the time, mingling with his shape, a half-shadow of a man, yet so real, with a burning heartbeat, in burning manly flesh, ready to open the her long and slender legs, and possess her as the woman he desired, uniting with her to become a living human being, in flesh and blood. He slowly touched her thighs and firm buttocks, gently kissing her half-open lips, whispering words she could only understand by listening intensely to his hot breath. With a little scream of desire, she could now feel his shadow becoming heavier, until she could feel his penis pressing hard against her pelvis. She wanted him to go on, already she was getting moist with pleasure, yet he wanted more of her wine, he wanted that secret spot to be wet, only for him. He took her hand, slowly guiding it along her waist and buttocks, to put it firmly between her legs. With a tight grip, he further parted them, pressing two of her fingers inside her. Yes, that felt so good, and she felt the wetness inside her, when he started to move her fingers to and fro. She knew he was observing her still, finding pleasure in her uncontrolled shivers, and the rhythmical movements of her body. He then put one of his fingers inside her, meeting her own, gently touching them, but pressing hard inside her, groping his way to touch that wet spot, that hard knot where all her desire culminated in pure lust and pleasure. She was holding her breath when he touched her there, slowly holding back, still, teasing her, until she took his hand wildly, to make him finish what he had started. She could feel his smile in the darkness, when he took her hand, putting it aside, to enter his finger inside her again, to massage her clitoris, gently at first, rhythmically, but then holding back to prolong her pleasure, touching her only slightly at the tip of her clitoris. His fingertip resting for a moment, he could feel that her wetness had transformed in that womanly juice that showed her need, her wish that he may enter her with his hard penis, but that would happen in another night, she knew, tonight he was there to give her pleasure by using his hand only. She felt crazy about that, yet she didn't want him to stop touching her there, again and again. It was that holding back that was making her want him even more, and again, she could feel his smile, when he concentrated on her clitoris with his massaging fingertip. He could feel it tighten and thicken, in anticipation of the climax. Then, shortly before she was bursting with desire, he took two fingers, gently taking her clitoris between the tips of his fingers, pressing hard, twisting slowly. He could feel the hard knob pulsating and crying out for more. He then just held her clitoris tight, pressing, leaving his fingertip hard on it. He could feel her bursting out, gasping, being trapped with her clitoris against his resting fingers, spurting out some wet drops of her orgasm against his fingers. Yes, he could feel her moisture, but without taking her with his hard and erect penis, he smiled in the dark. She could feel the weight of his body diminishing, and when she wanted to pull him into her arms, he was gone. Yet she knew he would be back, to give her pleasure again, and take her in whatever way she imagined him to...

<u>The Wolf</u>

Four years ago, I had been given a new chance. I had left the pack of wolves, I had stopped hunting for nightly prey that did not interest me too much. I had given up to get sick over too many sweet illusions that used to fill my heart for one night to end in desaster the next morning, when the softly glowing light of the Paris lantern that was shining into the window of my shabby apartment was switched off to let in the unpleasant light of truth. The grey muddy puddles on the sidewalk gloomily reflected my rugged and worn-out face while I bent forward to take a deep breath after another wasted night with a woman I hardly knew and surely did not love. I did not allow myself any weakness nor did I take an interest in following anyone and my dark self was the only thing that mattered, if there was anything that could be called holy in my forfeited life. Maybe that was why I was the type that women fell for in a last attempt to escape from the dullness of their lives to become at least aware of the fact that after all, there was a dark secret in themselves that had been replaced by romantic naivité for years yet still lay dormant like a dangerously encapsuled virus to burst out and infect their longing souls with lust and disorientation when they helplessly stared in my greyish intense and challenging eyes, only aware that this all was not a game after all but lethal reality to wake them up from sleeping in their rose gardens. I was their Prince, but the dark one, and I did not come to take them into my castle, but they were coming to me, I was calling them into my den, and it was too late when they realized that they had met the wolf, the real and bad one, the one that they desired most, to fill that emptiness in them up with unknown pleasures and some mysterious knowledge which would leave them forever changed and alone – and only the toughest of them would set out from that experience to start a new life, probably as a vampire, still unable to differentiate between sex and love, between truth and yearning, and soon, that hunting for love would turn more and more good guys into frustrated bad wolves like myself, yet they never would be able to leave the pack as they were poor followers, like their dark princesses that never became conscious, that after all, they still loved me, the lonely wolf, their eternal master.

But then I met her. And I worried. I ransacked my mind why she could not see the lost soul in me, the falsity, the wish to destroy, my low self-esteem. She truly loved me, and love sees everything. Then she must have known. But why on earth did she stay. She must have known that this was not part of the game, of my game. She made me want her, desire her with all my heart, with my entire body, and my manhood was pulsating in anticipation when I saw that caring and loving look in her honey brown eyes, naïve, yes, but womanly still, and it was too late when I discovered the horrible truth – that she became precious to me, even – holy. She posed a threat to me, for the whole show I had staged for the last years when I had given up on love and decided to go for vengeance. My heart bled, so I wanted a woman to bleed for me, to show womanhood that Eve should have never seduced Adam as the price was death and eternal loneliness until old age came and the awareness that the road they had taken had never led them to their homes. I felt my heart pounding with arousal and true joy when the doorbell rang and where a cold stone should have been, I could now feel a burning flame shooting through my groins igniting my balls with fire that were swelling like mad, even hurting against my tight jeans while I could feel my sharp brain going crazy. Her soft face looked like an angel, and I could not help but produce a hesitant smile, and I could hardly fight down the urge to force her down to the ground, part her legs gently, throw away her pair of satin slippers that she was wearing, and take her right there, in the doorway, without saying a word. I really wanted her, but the bad wolf in me was only put in a cage for a while, calmed down temporarily while the time bomb was ticking. I felt that cold sweat on my skin and when she touched my arms and said something I cannot even remember, I must have groaned in suppressed desire.

I went to the kitchenette, and for the first time I felt ashamed because of the shabbiness of my room, and the dirt on the furniture, the flimsy dark blue carpet, and I was thinking about the holes in the bedsheets, and the smell of the women that had spent the nights with me there, cheap women, helpless women, bored women, women that had made me throw them out the next morning to breathe in the virginity of the fresh morning air after the lantern lights had gone out again to give me hope for another lousy day in Paris.

While she was sipping the tea I had made for her, I was studying her fine neckline and somewhat stubborn chin, the rosy cheeks and thick eyelids with darkbrown lashes. She did not wear any makeup and if she did, it was not noticeable. The curve of her neck was elegant yet also vulnerable and her complexion was light and smooth like an

English rose that was accidentally planted next to rampant withering French weeds. I liked the way she gesticulated wildly with her small white hands that were naked without rings, the only jewels being her pale rose short and perfect fingernails. Her small mouth was soft and ruby red, and I wanted to touch it gently with my fingertips and kiss her wildly, while I could feel the wolve's growl silently rising inside me, getting more and more hungry, reminding me of my wild heart and my hardening penis that would soon spoil the stillness of that picture of beauty and longing to turn me into a creature of purely sexual and uninhibited lust that would push her against the wall, play wildly with her long dark hair to bite her neck and lips and tear open her light blue blouse to reveal the rounded flesh I was craving for. I imagined myself to pull up her neat short skirt and throw myself against her warm and moist pelvis while my hand was working its way underneath her lacy underwear to fill her up with three of my wanting and groping fingers. I wanted to move them in and out, feel the slickness and wetness of her vagina, feel the juice flowing, feel her getting ready for me, only for me. While I saw her lips moving and explaining something and that strange and surprised look in her eyes, I suddenly could not hold back my desire praying that the wolf inside me would understand me, and be tender and controlled. I was approaching her slowly, aware of her astonished and hesitating glance, after all, she must feel what I wanted, and that it was too late for her to leave. The wolf was warning me, yet I was still barking back at him threateningly, smiling at her warmly, yet my eyes must have been frozen, icy, full of anticipation and incalculability. I observed myself taking her hands, taking the cup of tea away from her, putting it softly back on the table. She was quiet now, insecure, yet understanding, indecisive, anxious, but also fascinated by my sudden approach. Run away, I prayed with my eyes closed, but listening to my heartbeat and the sweet pain between my legs, I told her to stay without words. Yes... She also was a follower, she stood up hypnotized, shivering, unable to look away from my yellow wolve's eyes. I could feel her skin exuding sweet sweat of desire, and I my sensitive sexual antennae noticed her willingness to yield, to give in to my warm mouth and hands that wanted to touch all of her, make her open her legs wildly under tiny and hoarse whispers that would soon grow into screams of pleasure when I took her hard and slow at first, then faster and heavy until both of us would not mind the wolf inside me any more as he had merged with the wild woman inside her to make her mine, forever united in that feeling of uncontrolled lust that yet would now only take her as she wanted to be taken, and had never known before. For a fraction of a second, I could see fear in her eyes, but then, her lips parted, showing her little tongue that started playing with mine, kindling that flame between my legs again, until I was pushing my knee forward right between her legs. I felt her slowly open them, waiting for me to carry on. While I was concentrating on her damp panties, she suddenly touched the bulge of my jeans, making me utter a short hard groan while I was grabbing her shoulders, pressing her hot soft body against my hardness. Like instinctive steps of a mysterious dance that only we two knew, she trailed backwards, guiding my hands along her waist, up to her small but full breasts. Her nipples were hardened and erect, I could see them poke against the thin fabric of her blouse. My sight was blurred, I was carried away by that pulsing blood in my veins, entranced by that hot feeling caused by her small hands pressing tightly against my bulge. She stood against the wall, her eyes closed, fumbling with my zipper, then opening it with a jerk. My penis was freed, big, thick, and hard, ready for penetration. I guided myself slowly into her, hearing her suppressed moans. While I was moving rhythmically to and fro, holding her around her waist while she leant against the wall, my teeth gently opened the top buttons of her blouse. I deeply sucked at her hard nipples that grew in my mouth like ripe raspberries. Squeezing her round breasts with one hand, I went down on her reaching her soft slender belly, gently massaging her flesh. I held my breath when she firmly gripped the root of my penis with both her hands, guiding me deeply inside her and out again, with her legs tightly pressed together. The wolf let go. That was too much for me, I could not hold back my orgasm any longer, and with wild and hard gusts, I spurted out into her, while she still was holding my penis. I could feel her come while I was inside her, her vagina muscles tensed around my penis, to make me stay hard for some more time. We finished, still holding each other, propped against the wall. My eyelids were quivering, I could feel her release, her body suddenly calm and sure. A soft touch of her fingertips made me open my eyes slowly. The dark brown velvet of her eyes were glowing, and there was some amber in it. I had not noticed that colour before, when she had sipped her tea. She smiled at me, her hands held tightly around my neck. "You are my wolf", she said.

When she had left, I went to the window, opened it, and leaned out to breathe in the fresh air of that new Paris morning. The lantern was still alight, its pale light throwing dancing shadows against the houses, and the muddy grey puddles of rainwater were moving wildly with the heavy drops falling down the dark and heavy clouds. I saw her downstairs, crossing the road, and without turning, she slowly walked out of sight.